The Best Baby-sitter in the World

by Marilyn Kaye

illustrated by Lauren Attinello

SCHOLASTIC INC.

New York Toronto London Auckland Sydney

For Rebecca and Anna Lee Burstein

ISBN 0-590-40703-1

Copyright © 1987 by Henson Associates, Inc.
All rights reserved. Published by Scholastic Inc.
THE MUPPET SHOW, MUPPET, and MUPPET character names are trademarks of Henson Associates, Inc.

HELLO READER is a trademark of Scholastic Inc.

12 11 10 9 8 7 6 5 4 3 2 1   7 8 9/8 0 1 2/9
                                                                    09
Printed in the U.S.A.
First Scholastic printing, April 1987

One sunny day,
Kermit called Fozzie Bear
on the telephone.
"Fozzie, please do a favor for me."

"Anything for you, Kermit,"
   Fozzie said. "What do you want?"

"I have a big problem," Kermit said.

"What kind of problem?" Fozzie asked.

"I saw a sign today. It said:

One frog needed to star in movie.

Tryouts at two o'clock."

"Wow!" said Fozzie.
"You could be a star!"

"But Robin is staying with me,"
Kermit said.
"I cannot leave him alone.
Will you baby-sit for Robin
while I am gone?"

"Baby-sit?" Fozzie asked.
"I do not know how to baby-sit!"

"Oh, please, Fozzie,"
 said Kermit.
"This is very important."

"But I never baby-sat before!"
 Fozzie said.

"Baby-sitting is easy,"
said Kermit. "I know
you can be the best baby-sitter
in the world!"

"But how?" Fozzie asked.
"What do I do with Robin?"

"Well, you can make cookies,"
Kermit said.

"That's easy," said Fozzie.

"You can play games," Kermit said.

"That's easy, too," said Fozzie.

"Maybe you can go to the zoo,"
Kermit said.

"Oh, boy!" Fozzie shouted.
"This sounds like fun!
I can do all that!
I can be the best baby-sitter
in the world! Okay, Kermit.
Here I come!"

"Fozzie is coming to baby-sit for you,"
  Kermit told Robin.

"But, Uncle Kermit,
  why do I need a baby-sitter?"
  asked Robin.
"I can take care of myself.
  I can be my own baby-sitter."

"No, you are still too young,"
  Kermit said.
"And Fozzie says he will be
  the best baby-sitter in the world.
  He can make cookies and play games.
  He can take you to the zoo."

"But I want to read my book,"
  Robin said.

Just then,
there was a knock on the door.

"Here I am!" said Fozzie,
"and I am so happy to be here!
It is time for fun, fun, fun
with Fozzie, the best baby-sitter
in the world!"

"You two have a nice day,"
Kermit said.
"I will be home at four o'clock.
Robin, be a good frog
and mind Fozzie. Okay?"

"Okay. Good-bye, Uncle Kermit."

"Now, what do you want to do first?"
Fozzie asked.

"I want to read my book," said Robin.

"Oh, no. We want to have fun,"
Fozzie said. "I know!
Let's make cookies!"

"Do you know how to make cookies?"
Robin asked.

"Oh, it is so easy," Fozzie said.
"All you need is flour and sugar
and butter and chocolate and nuts.
Then we throw it all together
and mix it up!"

Robin watched Fozzie.
In the bowl,
there was flour and sugar and
butter and chocolate and nuts.
But there was more on the floor.

"This is so wonderful!
I am having so much fun!"
Fozzie said.

"This is a mess,"
said Robin.

Fozzie put the cookies in the oven.

"What can we do now?" Fozzie asked.

"I want to read my book," said Robin.

"Oh, no," Fozzie said.
"We want to have more fun.
I know! Let's play hide-and-seek!
You hide. I will try to find you."

"Okay," Robin said.

Fozzie put his hands over his eyes.

Robin hid behind the sofa.

"One, two, three, four, five,"
Fozzie counted. "Here I come,
ready or not!"

He ran to the closet
and opened the door.

"I know you are in here!"
he shouted.
But Robin was not in the closet.

"I know! You are under the chair!"
But Robin was not under the chair.

"I know! You are behind the plant!"
But Robin was not behind the plant.

"Okay! I give up!
Where are you, Robin?"

"Here I am, Fozzie," Robin called.

"This is so much fun!" said Fozzie.

Robin looked around the room.

"This is a mess," he said.

Then he sniffed.

"Fozzie, I smell something funny."

The kitchen was full of smoke.
Fozzie opened the oven door.
All the cookies were burned.

"Oh, no!" Fozzie said.
"I left them in the oven too long.
But we can make some more."

Robin looked at the cookies.
What a mess!

"No, thank you, Fozzie," he said.
"I just want to read my book."

"No, no. We want to have more fun,"
said Fozzie. "I know!
Let's go to the zoo!"

"Do you know how to get there?"
Robin asked.

"Sure," said Fozzie.
"All the best baby-sitters know how
to get to the zoo."

They walked to the corner.

"First we have to cross the street,"
Fozzie said.

He stepped off the curb.
Robin grabbed his hand.

"Wait, Fozzie! The light is red!
You must not cross
until it turns green.
Then you must look both ways!"

"Oh, I guess I forgot that," Fozzie said.

After they crossed the street,
Fozzie stopped. He looked one way.
Then he looked the other way.
"I think we go this way," he said.

Robin pointed to a sign.
"No, Fozzie. We go that way,"
he said.

"You are pretty smart
for a little frog,"
said Fozzie.

At the zoo,
they saw a man selling food.

"Look at all the yummy stuff!"
Fozzie shouted. "I am so hungry!
Let's get hot dogs and cotton candy
and ice cream and popcorn!"

Soon Fozzie's arms were full of food.

"That's too much," Robin said.
"All that junk will make you sick!"

"I guess you are right,"
Fozzie said. "But I do not want
to waste all this food. I know!
Let's give it to the animals!"

Soda   .60
Ice Cream   .75
Hot dog   .50
Cotton Candy .75
Popcorn   1.00

SPECIAL
2 for
$1.00!

Fozzie took the food
to the lions' cage.

"No, Fozzie!" Robin yelled.
He pointed to the sign on the cage.

"Do not feed the animals,"
Fozzie read. "Oh, no.
Now what can I do with all this food?"

Just then, a lion roared.
Fozzie jumped in surprise.
Hot dogs and cotton candy and
ice cream and popcorn went flying
in the air.
Some of it landed on Fozzie.

"Look at you!" Robin said.
"You are a mess!"

Robin helped Fozzie clean up.

"Oh, I am so sorry, Robin,"
said Fozzie. "Thank you
for helping me."

"Do you want to go
to the monkey house?" Fozzie asked.
"I just love the monkeys.
They are almost as funny as I am!"

Robin saw a sign that read:
To the Monkey House.
"This way, Fozzie," he said.

Robin went into the monkey house.
"Look at that silly monkey, Fozzie,"
he said. But there was no answer.
"Fozzie? Fozzie, where are you?"

Robin ran all around
the monkey house.
But he could not find Fozzie.

Robin went up to the zookeeper.

"Mr. Zookeeper, I lost a bear. Did you see him?"

"No," said the zookeeper.

"But did you look in the bear house?"

"Good idea!" Robin said.

He ran to the bear house.

There was Fozzie.

He was telling jokes to the bears.

"Thank you, thank you, thank you.

I have a few more jokes.

Have you heard the one about — "

"Come on, Fozzie," Robin said.

"I think we should go home."

Robin watched out for Fozzie
all the way home.
He did not let Fozzie get lost.
He did not let Fozzie
buy any more food.
He made Fozzie wait
for the green light
to cross the street.

When they got home, Fozzie asked,
"Now, what can we do for more fun?
Do you want to bake more cookies?
Do you want to play more games?"

"Fozzie, I want to read my book,"
said Robin.

"But what can I do?"
asked Fozzie.

Robin gave Fozzie his book.
"Here, Fozzie.
You can read the book to me."

Fozzie started to read.
"Once upon a time,
there were three bears.
Oh, this is so good!
I love this story!"

Just then, Robin looked at the clock.
"Oh no! It is almost time
for Uncle Kermit to come home!
This house is a mess!
We have to clean it."

"But this book is so good,"
Fozzie said.
"I want to see how it ends!"
Fozzie kept on reading.

Robin went to work.
He cleaned up the kitchen.
He threw away the cookies.
He put all the clothes and toys
back in the closet.
He picked up the chair
and fixed the plant.

Just as Robin finished,
Kermit walked in the door.

"Hi, Uncle Kermit!
Are you going to be in the movie?"

Kermit shook his head.
"No, they said I was too green.
They picked a brown frog instead.
Hi, Fozzie.
How was your first baby-sitting job?"

"It was fun!" said Fozzie.
"I made cookies for Robin.
Then I played games with him.
I took him to the zoo, too."

"You were a good baby-sitter,"
Kermit said.

"Good?" Fozzie yelled. "I was great!
I was the best baby-sitter in the world!
Can I do it again sometime? Please?"

"Sure, Fozzie," Kermit said.
"See you later."

"Did you have a good time
with Fozzie?" Kermit asked Robin.

"It was okay," Robin said.
"But next time, I would like
to be my own baby-sitter."

"Could you do it?" Kermit asked.

"Oh, yes," Robin said.
"I learned something today.
I learned that I already know how to be—

the best baby-sitter in the world!"